THE
Cinderella Show

THE Cinderella Show

Janet and Allan Ahlberg

TOWN END
PRIMARY SCHOOL
presents

CINDERELLA

with

Narrator . . . . Anthony Narayan
Cinderella . . . . Tracey Hobbs
Stepmother . . . . Julie Dexter
The Ugly Sisters . . . . . Angelita Smith
                          Patricia Cutler
Prince Charming . . . . . Ramesh Patel
The Page . . . . Brian Ball
Fairy Godmother . . . Gillian Russell

The Clock . . . . Eric Potter
Two Horses . . . . . . Philip Hobson
                        Errol Pratt

DECEMBER 16th and 17th at 7.30.

ADMISSION 30p children 15p
Refreshments served in the hall

Sharon—
come back
here !

PUFFIN BOOKS

Published by the Penguin Group
Penguin Books Ltd, 80 Strand, London WC2R 0RL, England
Penguin Group (USA), Inc., 375 Hudson Street, New York, New York 10014, USA
Penguin Books Australia Ltd, 250 Camberwell Road, Camberwell, Victoria 3124, Australia
Penguin Books Canada Ltd, 10 Alcorn Avenue, Toronto, Ontario, Canada M4V 3B2
Penguin Books India (P) Ltd, 11 Community Centre, Panchsheel Park, New Delhi – 110 017, India
Penguin Group (NZ), cnr Airborne and Rosedale Roads, Albany, Auckland 1310, New Zealand
Penguin Books (South Africa) (Pty) Ltd, 24 Sturdee Avenue, Rosebank 2196, South Africa

Penguin Books Ltd, Registered Offices: 80 Strand, London WC2R 0RL, England

www.penguin.com

First published 1986
Published in this edition 2004
1 3 5 7 9 10 8 6 4 2

Copyright © Janet and Allan Ahlberg, 1986

Manufactured in China

British Library Cataloguing in Publication Data
A CIP catalogue record for this book is available from the British Library

ISBN 0-141-38094-2